I0740988

# Arco
## The legend of the blue vortex

**Ferdinando Manzo**

Publisher: Sydney School of Arts & Humanities
15-17 Argyle Place Millers Point NSW 2000
www.ssoa.com.au


ISBN: 978-0-9875961-9-2




Editing by Christine Williams

# Dedication

I dedicate this story to my grandfather Ferdinando …
Because, when I was five he showed me how amazing
Spider-Man, Tex Willer, Flash Gordon and so many
other characters of the imagination were.
Because, he taught me that, yes, there is another world
beyond the face you see in the mirror – you just have to
look into it.
Because, many years after he'd died he came back to
me. And when everyone was telling me, 'Mate, you
should change,' he said, 'Son, don't worry, just go for-
ward'.
So I did, Nonno. Yes, I did, and I do. Always.

# Acknowledgements

If someone tolerates you after such a long friendship and still helps you in your job – reading, editing, speaking, promoting, counselling you in the middle of the night because she lives on the other side of the world – well, you must say thanks, at the very least. So I'll do it. I'm actually doing it now …
…Thanks, Mariella Parmendola.


Thanks to my editor Christine Williams, whose hard and amazing work has allowed the vessel of Arco to proceed into the sea.

# Foreword

One evening over french fries and red wine, I met a journalist who carried the same dream that many journalists have tucked away in a drawer: to become 'a writer'. Now, Ferdinando Manzo has successfully opened that drawer and begun to climb the charts with his first novel, L'uomo che salvò il mondo. He's jumped from one side of writing to the other – from news to the novel – a move which had its baptism in conjunction with the author's journey from Naploli to Australia. A flight halfway around the world – that's nothing compared to the journey that Ferdinando takes his readers on, those readers who decide to immerse themselves in his stories, the first a novel set in an apocalyptic scenario of post nuclear war, and the second a short story of a journey by Arco in search of 'the blue vortex'. This short story, published in English, is a lucky chance that Ferdinand has taken along with his publisher, Sydney School of Arts and Humanities. For a dip in the fantasy genre, between unhappy love and underwater worlds, the writer goes to the extreme, abandoning his news writing style so that he can give his readers a quite different experience. As a professional journalist, Ferdinando took his first steps in crime reporting at the same newspaper, Metropolis, where I'd worked for many years, in an era different from his. In fact, that's not where we met, but, rather, through mutual friends one evening when we found ourselves sitting in a pub drinking wine and eating fries. And talking about journalism, writing, dreams, and travel. It's been a while since then ... and now some of the dreams have become a reality.

**Bruno De Stefano**
*'Newton Compton editore' author*

My story dates back many years. At that time I was a carefree and besotted youth wanting to enjoy the freedom offered by a world apparently more sincere, so different from the one we live in now, unfortunately, as I have come to know it.

I loved a woman. She was beautiful. She was gentle. She had a sweet name and a hot temper. She was a combination of sensuality and beauty. She danced with elegance in a body made of stunning and proportionate curves covered with casual clothes, which highlighted her beauty without seeming excessive. What most attracted me was her reserved character that she hid, and was only seen by those who knew how to spy discreetly. She had a passion outside of the common. The first time I saw her half-naked, we were on a lawn in the moonlight. Under a big tree that partially hid our bodies. I touched and kissed her velvety breasts. I felt an emotion I would never feel again.

Later, at the lowest point in my life I met a weathered man in a bar.

'If you wanna finish a bottle of whiskey, talk to someone and keep drinking. But if you are alone, as I am, just tell a story.'

Yes. He said something like that, but it was a long time

ago and he is not here now. No one is here now. I'm alone, just as he was. I'm alone with my past, with my present, with my bottle of whiskey. Yes. I do want to finish it tonight. And as there is no one with me to speak to, I'll tell you my story. The story of my life, of his life. The story of Commander Arco, of my ship, of the blue vortex. Of my love.

She was my first, unique, great love. She came into my life breaking up my ideas and erasing an image of myself that I had built through difficulties in my mind. This love tale was a consummated story within a few months, rushing to a climax. It was a wind of passion that never subsided.

The era we lived in was one when emotions had to bend to the will of weapons. They were years of conflict that tormented Europe and showed the world the horror of war and the wickedness of men. We parted, not of our own will, but only because of the obligation dictated by duty, the call to war. But our love continued to live in memory, without a smudge. Not a single negative thought could overshadow that story. Not a single doubt affected our desire to come back together.

I was obliged to take up the rifle and march to defend my land from the invasion and arrogance of those who were wreaking havoc on the continent and spreading a barbarism that was mortifying man in his innermost essence.

For too many years the hissing of bullets replaced the sweet whisper of her words of love. For too many years, the explosions and flames of the bombs, replaced our nights of passion under the stars. I would have given up that uniform, that rifle, that knife and gone back to her. To her love. To our love. But I could not.

When death danced around us, as it did around tens and hundreds of soldiers in the trenches or in the occupied streets of our city, I thought only of her. I resisted and struggled against the exterminating angel because I wanted to, I had to, go back to her. There was no other thought in my mind than that of her delicate skin that touched my body as I touched her hair.

When the war ended, I looked for her. It wasn't easy to get to her country. Roads, railways, everything was in ruins, destroyed or damaged. Few homes remained and entire villages were razed to the ground. In spite of everything, I was able to find her family, and the day I knocked on the door of a red house with a sloping roof, I almost couldn't believe my eyes. The woman who opened the door had a delicate face with a sweet and unmistakable expression. Her mother seemed to have aged fifty years, but she was still beautiful. She told me that her daughter had enlisted as a volunteer nurse because she hoped to meet me at the front, but, instead, she'd been sent to the other side of Europe to serve her country, working for a religious organisation that cared for the injured.

I started walking. I marched incessantly until I reached the town where the organisation's head office was to be found. From there I was sent to another country, because my love seemed to have become a volunteer in a convent in the south.

I went on, without losing heart. I was happy walking towards that goal, which I felt coming closer. I walked for days, sleeping a few hours each night and marching from dawn to dusk.

Finally, I reached the address that was given to me by the headquarters. What I found there wasn't reassuring. At all.

The convent had collapsed, destroyed by bombing over previous months. There were only a few stones to tell the story of that ancient building that had for so long withstood the disasters of the times but, ultimately, not the madness of men. It was there I met a nun. She was praying just a short walk from the wreckage where once had stood the altar of the chapel. The woman was over seventy yet she had dug for days on end, between dust and stones, in an attempt to rescue the survivors of the massacre, and then to recover the bodies of the dead, to give them a dignified burial. She told me the truth of a senseless tragedy that had no explanation, even in those years of absurd madness where men had learned to live like beasts.

My beloved was saved. Her body had remained under the rubble for days before being found by rescue workers. They picked her up and she was still breathing. Her heart had not given up. And I thought that she could never give up, because she had a purpose: she was waiting for me. She couldn't die before we'd seen each other. One more time.

The hospital where they had taken my beloved was a day and a half's journey away. Again I walked for hours. Then … I had to stop. Fatigue halted me. My tired legs had ceased responding to my desperate eagerness. So I threw myself on the ground, and rested between nightmares and cold chills which agitated my sleep. That night brought with it an omen of misfortune. Before dawn illuminated the streets, I was already on my way to the hospital. Down the footpath I went, first marching then running like a madman until I arrived outside a gate to a building that stretched along the south side of a hill. I stepped through the wrought-iron gate, decorated with the shapes of snakes intertwined through its bars, and I walked toward the majestic wooden door that marked the entrance. Along a narrow white corridor, I met a nurse, her face showing the strain she was under – cheeks hollowed and dark circles under her eyes. I asked her if the woman I loved was there. In which room? What was her condition? I received no reply. Just a gesture: I saw the nurse's right hand rise up slightly, her finger trembling, to show me a stretcher.

I had arrived too late. My love had been dead for just a few hours. She was at rest, covered in a white sheet that showed only her feet. My trek had been in vain.

On that day, at that moment, my world died. I died. Without her, nothing would make any sense again. My life no longer had a purpose. For years I had lived with her alone in my memory, in the hope that our love could finally burn with a new passion. In the hope that one day death would come, putting an end to our happy old age together. I couldn't resign myself to the idea of losing her, that I had not been able to reach her in time, that I had not seen her smile. At least one last time. I had promised her I'd be back and that I would never abandon her. I had given her my word, as a pledge of my love. But I had betrayed that promise.

Her funeral was attended by two nuns on duty at the hospital and a faded image of myself, paralysed with pain. I looked like a scarecrow battered by crows and at the mercy of the wind. I managed to place a small bunch of cream freesias on her coffin, before spadesful of moist earth covered her, the fresh grave bare of any grass.

I spent whole days in that cemetery that continued to expand with the victims of the war. Despite the guns being silenced by peace treaties, the land continued to be nourished by the blood of the wounded and maimed, those still wearing a brand of horror.

I spent sleepless nights interspersed by continuous obsessive dreams, another spectrum of reality, whether prescient or just a mirror of my altered mood. I've never understood it. I tried to remedy that state of mind which made my rest a fatigue even worse than my daily struggle for survival, but there was no way out. I didn't want to abandon my memories. I couldn't resign myself to losing her forever. Often I slept near the house of the caretaker of the cemetery and during the day I spent my time leaning on my love's headstone.

When my discomfort was at its peak, I would abandon momentarily the cemetery and wander in the woods. I would contemplate the cliffs, thinking that I wanted to throw myself over them. I walked desperately between beaten tracks and steep fields, without a destination. Then, one day, I decided to move away, to give up that hill and follow unknown roads. I walked without stopping, and aimlessly. I wandered off the beaten track, where only a few months earlier, soldiers had made those woods their home quarters. I don't know how, but in the end I found myself, and it was in a pub.

In that infamous but cosy place I met an old man. A fisherman. That man changed my life.

When I entered, he was sitting on a stool next to the bar. He was alone and had a dark expression on his face. His gaze never deviated from a glass of whiskey, his only companion, despite the fact that the local was full of people. I walked over to the bar and asked for a drink. Then the old man came over to me, to strike up a conversation.

'Are you a military guy?'

'Yes,' I replied, 'a sailor.'

'And what brings you to this place, sailor?'

'Nothing. I came here, and nothing else. Without a reason,' I replied in such a low voice that I doubted he would hear me.

'Perhaps there is a reason. There is always a reason, sailor. What do you say about offering an old fisherman something to drink?'

I looked him straight in the eye. And his look, though surly, seemed anything but bad. It was that of a man abandoned to a lonely existence. Maybe he just needed to talk with someone. In that place I had no friends, and I had no desire to make new friends. But something in him was different. I felt him close to me, my equal. A man devoured by suffering perhaps equal to mine. So I didn't hesitate.

'Why not? But I'm tired of standing up. Come on, we can sit there. From that table you can see the ocean.'

We moved. He followed me, dragging his left leg. His limp showed some sign of an injury that still gave him pain. Just like for so many others. At that time, the war had scarred those who had not been killed.

We ordered a bottle of whiskey. The waiter brought it to us with two small glasses and I poured a drink for us both. I sipped my drink. He drank his down in one gulp. Then he filled his glass again.

'I want to tell you a story. A true story,' he said, after drinking his third glass.

'It's a story only known by a few that is handed down as a legend fuelled by old men of the sea. It's a truth that is incredible and mysterious.'

So saying, he took another shot of whiskey and began his story.

'There is a place in the vast blue sea where currents coming from the four cardinal points intersect. They merge into a single vacuum, canceling each other out. It's a place where the water becomes immobile and is an intense deep blue, devoid of color variations. This place is called the blue vortex. The vortex is a place where there is no bottom. They say that it is the heart of the sea, the source that generates life, the place where it all began, where every form of life originates. No one knows where it is located, yet seafaring legends have handed down this myth since the beginning of history. It is said that someone was able to discover it by following a map traced by the stars and, charmed by the beauty of that vision, he dived deep down inside it during a night of the full moon and never returned. Many have died trying to find him, deceived by the hope of eternal life, which the blue vortex seems to offer.

The cult of this place reached a high point around the time that pirates ruled the high seas, when finding its whereabouts became the mission of the most intrepid captains who sailed between the coasts of the two continents.

According to legend, only one man was capable of reaching that place. He was Commander Arco, a young and inexperienced sailor who formed a crew composed of novices of the sea and people from the pubs who had been banned from working any vessel. His ship sailed from the coast of Spain one June night. No one heard from the vessel until fourteen months later, when one of its lifeboats reappeared in port. Of Commander Arco and more than half of his crew, there was no trace. The story of what had occurred has been handed down through tales of pirates who left the sea forever, after that experience.

The story goes that Arco found himself in the middle of the ocean after a terrible storm blew him off course. He faced a sea that no sailor could remember ever having seen in his life. Mountains of water hit the ship, which seemed destined to capsize at the mercy of the raging wind and rain. The sailors were forced to bind themselves to any object that offered some guarantee that they would not be swallowed up by eddies of foam as the air sucked at everything. Stocks of food ended up in the sea, and the wood of the ship seemed to creak under its blows. No one knows how long the hellish storm lasted. It is said that the sky remained dark for several days, perhaps a week. When the crew came to its senses the ship floated, battered but intact, to an unknown point in the ocean. It was in the middle of a kind of motionless lagoon, where there was neither current nor wind. The vessel was stagnant on the blue vortex. Unwittingly, it had reached its goal.

The pirates, enraptured, stood watching the show and then, under the silvery rays of a full moon so bright, Commander Arco gave them the order to tie together the longest sheets on the ship. He made the crew tie one end of a sail to the top of the main mast and then wrapped the other end around his hips. Then he put a cannonball in a net and tied it to his belt. He demanded to be thrown into the sea and then rescued as soon as the sailors felt a three-times tugging of the rope. That would be the signal for the Commander, freed of the cannonball, to be swiftly pulled up on board the ship by his men to avoid drowning. But no one was to pull the rope until they'd received the order. Such an act would be considered insubordination and for the guilty there would be capital punishment, he said.

The crew obeyed. Commander Arco was thrown into the sea with his cannonball. Eternal seconds passed. One sailor swore that he counted over two hundred, and everyone was sure of the captain's death, before the signal came. The captain was rescued. His body was laid on the deck of the ship. Amazingly he was still dry, with not even a drop of water dripping from his clothes. He looked dead, but he wasn't.

When he opened his eyes, they were the same colour as the moon. His face had changed and seemed more mature, devoid of that carefree air, that ruthlessness mixed with a student spirit, that his youth gave him. He jumped up and looked around, staring at his men one by one, without a word. Reaching the navigation bridge, he put his right foot on the carved wood railing, where half-naked mermaids supported a balustrade little more than an inch wide. He called his men and passionately told them from on high what he had seen: in the blue vortex there was a world! A world inhabited by humans and creatures never seen before, of shapes and colours unknown. A world in which we breathed and spoke just as we did above sea level. There were houses, and palaces of white marble covered with gold and precious stones that sparkled and reflected in dancing bubbles, transported by mild ocean currents. On the sinuous streets paved with white stones, there were musicians and poets, dancers and writers, and charming women dancing with fish. There Arco had met a man of advanced age, with a statuesque physique with a silvery beard to his navel. He spoke without opening his mouth. But Arco could feel him, he understood his language and caught each word he spoke in a tone devoid of accents and cadences, but solemn. From the lips of that old man, no words came out, no sound. Nothing. He was holding in his right hand a transparent crystal lamp in which shone a light blue flame that emanated no heat.

"You don't need a tool to produce a sound. You don't need ears to listen to it, nor a mouth to sing. Don't be surprised. This is not your world. Here is not a reflection of light that comes from an unknown location. Here the light is of life. Here is  life which will become light. Light is our very essence – it flows between water molecules in the bodies of creatures that inhabit this world, in rocks, algae, anything. Everything you see is life, and is light. The sensations you feel, the music you listen to, the pictures you see, everything you can sense is light. Everything exists in light. As well as everything you don't know about. Come with us. This is a place where time doesn't exist, where what is dead is reborn and what is alive never dies, but continues to live in the flame of eternity. In this place there is no hatred, only love."

"I'm ready," Arco replied, enchanted by that magical land and the words of his keeper.

Devil or angel, whoever it was, the old man had persuaded the Commander. So Arco slipped the dagger from his belt and tried to cut the rope that bound him to the ship. But he couldn't. That blade, so sharp that the surface was able to penetrate into the flesh of a man as if it was warm butter, was not able to cut the rope that had become harder than a metal chain.

"You can't break it, or cut it," said the guardian of the blue vortex. "It is the law of our world: those who want to live here have to do it by choice, and the choice must be free, independent and final. You can change your world but to do it you will not have any more ties with the past. That which is above the surface will remain there. When you jumped from the ship you decided to tie yourself to a rope to be rescued and to return to your world. You've been holding on to what you have. Fear of the unknown and of losing what you have, these have not made you free – and now you can't cut this rope. You can only rise to the surface and make your choice. If you want to return here you will have to free yourself from the burden of your past. You'll have to throw yourself into the sea without fear or remorse, and plunge into the current that will take you to a new life. Only then will you be accepted in our world. Forget fears. Forget what binds you to another person. Free your mind from the constraints of a culture that had you locked up in a society of customs, traditions and beliefs that imprison the spirit. Expand your cosmos, so that it blends with the water that flows motionless in this sea, and with the different creatures that live in the harmony of the blue light. Only in this way will you be free to choose. Go, go now. Go back to your world and make your choice."

Arco's story excited the crew. The captain pulled out his sabre, cut the rope that bound him to the main mast and jumped about the ship. He screamed enough to tear his vocal chords, as if he wanted to send his voice to the deepest depths of the sea.

"I have chosen. I have chosen. Men, be architects of your own fate. If you follow me, I will show you paradise. I will give you a new life. I will give you immortality."

He jumped off the ship, clutching a cannonball in his arms. But none of his crew followed him. Through cowardice or good sense, everyone preferred to stay on the ship. They waited until the end of the night, staring into the water, waiting for Arco's lifeless body to appear, but they saw no one re-emerge from the depths, either alive or dead.

And when the moon moved away, and the sea was illuminated by the rays of the rising sun, the sky became a covering of dark clouds. Another terrible storm came upon them, and the ship couldn't resist this time. It split into two pieces and fell to the nadir of the open sea, where shortly before, there had been a blue vortex. Some of the sailors were able to store some water for themselves in a lifeboat before another storm swept them away. The others had no way out; they couldn't escape from the fury of the waves that carried them off somewhere, turning them into food for sharks.

When the survivors recovered and found themselves in the open sea, they believed they had had a dream. There was no trace of Commander Arco and most of the crew. The group resumed their navigation, wandering across the ocean until they were rescued by a cargo ship that followed a route back from America. So it was that they managed to return to Spain, and to report the incident.'

'Stop telling stories, old man,' broke in the voice of the

innkeeper as he arrived at the table to pick up the glasses and empty bottle.

'If you continue to tell these legends, sooner or later someone will believe you.'

He laughed, looking around while people at the other tables seemed to sneer, pleased at his words.

But the old man didn't flinch. Sitting with arms folded, he looked at me and said,

'Don't listen to the words of those who believe or don't believe based only on ignorance or superstition, sailor. Unfortunately we are not able to give or receive the answers we seek, but that doesn't mean that they don't exist.'

'Bring us another bottle, please,' I said to the innkeeper.

'First the money, then the whiskey, is the way it works here.'

'Here's your money,' I told him.

'Whether the existence of the blue vortex is truth or legend, sailor, I cannot say,' continued the old fisherman, showing his appreciation for the new bottle which had arrived at the table with a curt nod.

'What is certain is that there is a note in the Spanish historical archives of a Commander Arco, presumed lost at sea when he was still very young. Then there is another thing that I haven't said yet.'

'What is it?'

'The lifeboat on which the survivors were found, still exists and is proof of that journey.'

'And how do you know?'

'Simple. I know because I'm its guardian. I found it long ago, after years and years of research. It was moored in the suburbs of a port, abandoned among wreckage. I bought it for very little money and I brought it here.'

'And how can you be sure that it is that lifeboat?'

He smiled, bringing another glass of whiskey to his lips.

'I know because that dinghy has belonged to my family since it returned from the sea after the disaster. An ancestor of mine was part of the crew of Commander Arco and he jealously guarded that boat. For generations it was a family treasure, then it remained lost up until about 1800, when it was sold by one of my spendthrift ancestors who had a gambling addiction. To pay a debt, he sold the lifeboat that was by then a collector's item. But for some reason, at the beginning of this century all that was ancient was considered just useless waste. In this way, the boat was first abandoned at the port, then on a construction site, and then somewhere on the coast, where I found it.'

'Fascinating history. And after so many years, it is still able to navigate?'

'Don't be silly, of course. Years ago I personally restored it, but now it would need to be made seaworthy and I have no intention of doing that.'

'Why not? It might be good business for you. You might be able to sell it.'

'I don't think so. And the reason is simple: my ancestor decided to jealously preserve that dinghy and didn't put it back into the sea because its soul might have been drawn towards the blue vortex.'

'How? What does that mean? I don't understand.'

'Believe it or not, boats have a soul, a heart. All seamen see their legendary reputation alongside that of their own ship. And this is not a coincidence, but only proof of the indissoluble relationship that is created between a captain and his vessel. In that lifeboat is locked up the soul of the ship that sank and is perhaps still on the seabed, where the blue vortex appeared.'

'But if you believe this story, why not try to find the great vortex, instead of staying here to drink, and get drunk, and slowly kill yourself?'

The old fisherman's face suddenly darkened, as if the clouds of a summer storm had obscured the sun. He put the glass down on the table with a nervousness that swelled the veins of his face so that a long blue groove appeared on his skin, dried by years of intense sun and salt. Without raising his eyes, he stared at his glass as if watching images of his life scroll across its base. Holding the glass with thumb and forefinger, he swung it about so that the few drops of alcohol in the bottom created a wave. The light in his eyes during his telling of the story of Arco disappeared, leaving them dark, with his lids half-closed.

'The dagger of memory has armed my pains to become the executioner of my heart and the guillotine of my spirit. I have sunk into the abyss of a time long gone and lost to the edge of an isolated galaxy, in which gravitate only sorrow and resignation. Why should I deprive myself of alcohol, the only pleasure that soothes thoughts and sorrows chained to memory? What death could be worse than being consumed by pain? It's the generator of vortices of regrets and false confessions, a mirror of a reality distorted by time, a deceptive illusion. No, sailor. There could be no worse condemnation. There could be no more excruciating torture than that which devours your flesh from the inside, biting you with sharp fangs of regret and poisoning you through guilt, to take over your existence, trapping it in a timeless oblivion. What torture could be worse than that sense of emptiness that takes possession of your life, destroying every little emotion, turning you into a leaf at the mercy of the wind? None. No death could be worse than the slow and excruciating. That's why, in this torture, I prefer to watch the play of derisory shadows which assist me daily, overwhelming me with the passion that only alcohol can give. Look. Look at those houses there ...'

'Beyond the grove,' he said, still staring at the glass.

'Watch them well and carefully. In those buildings that you see, there is enclosed a part of my life that I can't drive off and that continues to haunt me every day. Every night. I see again those pictures in every moment of my existence reflected everywhere, even in this sky so sadly full of rain and devoid of wind, dominated by clouds that look so heavy as to keep on raining until they join with the sea. No knife can ever be more sharp and pungent than this memory that pierces my heart every day. Sailor, you may claim not to have yet become an old drunk, crazy from alcohol abuse, just as customers of this bar make that claim about me. They judge me, without appeal. They pass judgment without taking into account the complexity of another's existence, only using the measure of the normality and banality of themselves. They look at me with eyes blinded by prejudice and conditioned by the criteria that their selfish personal systems impose on consciences empty and impregnated with indifference. They live in their own little world of unconscious acceptance, locked in a dimension so small that it turns them into a giant inanity. If you look around, you'll see them jabbering and laughing: waving their beer mugs, talking excitedly, challenging each other in stupid competitions, and laughing at me. But I don't care about them. I let them think what they want. Basically, they need to take time out too. Who cares if they do it, whether by laughing at me, someone else or themselves? At one time, perhaps, I would have laughed too. At one time I would have done so many things. I too wanted to sail the seas with my woman, leave the shore with her in search of the blue vortex. That's the reason that prompted me to restructure the dinghy, years ago. I prepared it for the trip. I spent many years and much money to renovate the lifeboat so that it could accommodate two people, living on board for quite a long time. My desire was to leave with her and arrive at the place that would preserve our love from the deterioration that time would inevitably imprint on our bodies. I would have liked to get to that place to dance with her forever, to live an eternal day of love that knew neither dawn nor sunset.'

I watched him and listened to the nostalgic flavour of his words, seeing in him a different man than I'd imagined. At that moment in front of me, there wasn't an old drunk fisherman who told legends to young sailors. No. At that moment at the table sat a man who was stripped of his mask. He was naked and uninhibited, opening a chest kept closed for many years, a chest in which he kept his sorrows still shining.

'What happened? Why didn't you go?' I asked him in a tone of compassion, waiting for an answer that I wasn't convinced I wanted.

'One day,' he continued in his narrative, staring into the bottom of the glass, 'coming home from the yard where I'd been restoring the boat, I couldn't find her anymore. She had vanished. Had disappeared from my life just as suddenly as she had appeared. I searched for her everywhere for a long time. I wandered in the darkness, until one day I found her. I'd dreamed of that encounter so many times that I had memorised all the things I wanted to say to her, to express what I felt and thought. But when at last the time came, I found myself totally unprepared. Like a young boy and his first time. I realised that there is no preparation. There is no prediction. When the important time comes, you're alone. In doubt and pain. But if instead there is joy, there is always someone ready to share it with you. The world thrives on selfishness. This is the truth, a truth that may seem cynical and pessimistic, but it is not. It's only a truth that you just get used to, like drinking a bottle of whiskey before going to bed. I knew it that day, when I saw her, long after the end of our story. I followed her to a bar and, inside, I grabbed her by the arm. She turned and looked at me. It was then that I walked away without looking back. I didn't even have the courage to talk to her once I'd looked into her eyes. Their expression was not the brightness of love, but was cold and sharp like darts of ice. My hell began that day. I went back home, but the desert that I carried inside me even dried up the streets on which I walked. Murmurs that previously had had a familiar sound became trumpets of oppression, unbearable. Everything was grey and cold and nothing made sense to me, not even the journey that I'd wanted to undertake. To reach the vortex would have made my suffering eternal. That was why I decided to move to this island, leaving everything that I had been on the other shore. I brought only the boat with me. My family treasure, the only thing that tied me to the world. I attempted to forget, to remove the past from my mind, to free my thoughts obsessed by memory. But I couldn't, because that time that I'd lived had not abandoned me, and even now it continues to pursue me, to wear me down.'

'Yours is a sad story,' I said simply, without meaning the words to come out of my mouth.

'No, it's just a life story. A real story, like many others. Maybe it has nothing special, maybe it's a story that you'll soon forget, and besides, you wouldn't even have reason to remember it. But look ... the bottle is almost empty.'

'Another, please?' I asked the waiter who then spoke with the barman.

The face of the fisherman which had become even more shadowy in the reflection of the empty bottle, lit up when the whiskey was poured into his glass. And savouring that dark nectar, he continued his story of twenty years earlier as if a mysterious crowd was gathered there to watch him and follow his words:

'A dark cloud envelops my heart, so that it's long been incapable of loving. Everything around me seems lifeless, empty and inadequate. Since moving here I have lived only for apathy. I live in harmony with sea and whiskey, because there is nothing else to comfort me as I wait for the end.'

I felt sorry for that man who, despite his advanced age, was continuously dying, not through illness, but from a slow and excruciating monotony of an empty existence, of years lived drifting through the distorting lens of a bottle. His story had surfaced in me all the grief over the death of my love, so I stood up, moved to the bar to pay, and I left enough money on the counter for another bottle that the old man could drink the next day. Then I walked back to farewell him.

'Remember,' he said, raising his glass of whiskey, 'that when sadness assails you as you lean against a bar, you will understand how deep your hell. When you see an empty bottle and your arm raised to ask for another, you will understand that there is no end, even if you continue to hope to the contrary. And when the voices that surround you become a distant echo and you feel about yourself the emptiness of your existence that can't be filled by alcohol, then you'll start to look back, repenting everything you were not, yet wanted to be. A sense of helplessness assails you and you realise that you can't be the arbiter of your life, that even your desires are repressed by fear of others' judgments and the inability to be accepted by the world. At that moment you can't do anything but grab a glass and swallow. Hoping that sooner or later the alcohol will overwhelm your thought.'

When I left the bar a light rain was falling and the village was enveloped in misty lamplight along its wide boulevards. The smell of burning oil hit my nostrils as the aroma wafted in the air. It reminded me of nights spent on the battlefield behind the trench, a lamp burning in our small and crowded military tent, as I listened to the notes of a harmonica helping to exorcise our fear. A fear that danced like a spectrum in a gloomy night atmosphere marked by the outbreak of mortars, when silence would have been the only reassuring voice. In that air, full of the smell of gunpowder and sweat, with skin chapped by the wind and our wounds caked with dried blood, lamp oil reminded me temporarily of my family hearth. That war had tied up our lives, and we feared the horror of our distant homes being uninhabited, or worse yet, destroyed.

As I wandered through the streets, rain penetrated my clothing, cooled by a cold wind that blew in from the sea. Then I found a place to rest, sleeping under the awning of a closed shop. I was not safe but I didn't care.

That night my dreams were more restless than ever before. Yet, for the first time, I saw a glimmer of light in a faded image: a sail. A sail in the wind dragging me away to float on water of such an intense blue as to dazzle the gulls engaged in aerobatics across the horizon.

The next morning I went back to the pub early and found that old fisherman already drinking, downing glasses of whiskey that the bartender served him from a bottle to the side of the bar. When the old man saw me, he gave a bitter smile and motioned to me that he knew the alcohol was my gift from the night before.

I walked over to the fisherman, grabbed him by the arm and pulled him outside, even grabbing the bottle from the counter.

On the beach, the sun's rays were a blinding light which perhaps even he no longer remembered as he was drowning in litres of alcohol. He dropped like a dead weight as soon as I loosened my grip, collapsing among the sand dunes, with their grassy ridges a natural barrier between the bay and a series of hills, six hundred metres behind. Away to the east was a small village, with customs and traditions different from those of the fishermen, who lived a few hundred metres to the west of the bay.

I pushed and I pulled the old man back down the beach into the shallows, hoping that the wind blowing cold air from the hills towards the sea would help him throw off his hangover. Or at least it would give me the opportunity to explain to him the reason for my visit so early in the morning.

'I need your boat, old man. Can you hear me? I need your boat. Come on, look at me. I have to find the blue vortex and I need your help.'

I tried to throw him face first into the sea water. But I saw that I had some time to wait before he would recover.

'He drank all night without ever straying from the bottle,' I heard a voice call out.

'When I returned for the morning shift, he was still at the table with his glass full, and he only left off when he'd finished it. He asked me for another whiskey and I opened the bottle you'd paid for last night.'

The waiter, who was watching me from the bar's doorway as he pretended to sort the garbage bags, wasn't trying to justify the excessive amount of alcohol that he'd served, he was only telling me so I'd understand that the old fisherman was unlikely to sober up anytime soon. So I asked him if he knew where the fisherman was staying.

Then I dragged him home, exhausted by the time I'd arrived.

In his dimly lit room that smelled of old age and rising damp, I found the old man's bed and laid him on it. His blankets spilled onto the floor, which was covered with empty bottles and cans dripping beer. I left him there to rest while I searched the two-roomed house for a glass of water. The stove and sink were blackened by filth and years of rust, with crusts of dirt that would never come off, even with the most powerful acids on the market. Water dripped from the oxidized tap, forming a brownish pool in the sink in which floated leftovers of the same food that encrusted soaking dishes. The vision of that scene convinced me that the only feasible way to satisfy my thirst would be to drink directly from the tap.

Time passed, accompanied by the sound of the hands of an old clock on the wall. I waited and watched the sea which reflected that spring day's golden sunshine, until the heavy, close air of the house became unbearable. I decided to go outside for a respite from the stench that even the open windows couldn't quell.

As I walked along the beach, I saw a hut completely covered by climbing plants clutching it in large clumps of tangled branches. I approached with curiosity. A heavy bolt was blocking another bolt made of iron. I tried to find a crack that would allow me to look into the hut inside the forest of wood and grass, on which the sun spread shades of gold. But it was useless. Not a single ray of light penetrated beyond the wall. This had to be the place where the boat was guarded, I thought. I went back to the door and tested the strength of the deadlock which, unlike anything I had seen up to that time in the house, was neither old nor dirty. Indeed, it seemed to be cleaned on a regular basis. I tried to force it with a stick, but that didn't help. I needed the key. And, just when I felt a sudden despair flatten the hope that I'd had all morning, a hand grabbed my arm and pushed me away from the entrance.

'Give me some space. If you want to get in there, you'll have to use this!'

It was the old fisherman, who was finally sober and had brought me the key to open the lock. He turned it with a certain firmness and strength, then he pulled the bolts open and took them off, hanging them on a nail protruding from the wall. He opened the door slowly, exerting enough pressure to swell his neck veins as he fought against the soil and rocks that hindered the door's movement.

'Here … this is what you are looking for.'

I looked with awe and respect, feeling an intense energy that attracted me toward what for me had become a relic with supernatural powers, able to perform the miracle that I believed in dogmatically. I closed my eyes and stepped across the threshold of the cabin. Finally I saw it. A beauty! Its broad keel stood majestically upon the ground supporting a skeleton of wood that smelled antique yet glistened like new. The boat's edge was smooth and fresh as if it had never suffered from the past.

'It's all original wood,' said the fisherman, satisfied on seeing the admiration in my eyes. I was in ecstasy. Struck by Stendhal syndrome, that sensation of dizziness, confusion or rapid heartbeat when struck by a vison of personal significance, I felt as if I was immersed in an hallucination.

'Come on, now,' said the old man, pulling me back to his home and pushing me toward the side of the cabin where there was a table, the same type as those at the pub.

'Sit down here.'

He opened the door to a shelf and pulled out a bottle of whiskey. Then two glasses. He filled them and sat down, took a drink and looked at me.

'So … tell me why I should give you my ship and why you want to get to the blue vortex.'

'Because I want to go,' I told him, paraphrasing his quote of the night before, 'to the place where time doesn't exist, where what was dead is reborn and what is alive never dies, but continues to live in the flame of eternity.'

We spent hours sitting at that table. He continued to drink and I continued to talk incessantly, telling him the story of my life and my lover who had died a few weeks before.

'I'll help you,' promised the fisherman, after listening to me as he consumed half a bottle of whiskey.

'Do what you need to do. Meanwhile, I will prepare the boat. When you come back here all you'll need to do is just go to sea.'

I believed in his words and in his willingness to help me. I knew he was sincere. The old man saw in me the young man he had been and had tried to forget. He never said this, but I felt that in his heart he fervently hoped that my mission would succeed and I would realise my dream. A dream we shared.

I left the house, my heart filled with joy, and I walked to the cemetery where my love was buried. The dark mantle of night had already enveloped the small cemetery, lost in the silence of the hills, where the echo of goat bells was the only annoyance to the eternal repose of the dead.

When the time came, I began to dig with all the strength I had in my body until the steel of my spade struck the wood of the coffin. Using my bare hands, I wiped its lid clean of soil. When I opened the coffin, I saw her face smiling. She was happy. She hadn't expected this other me. I lifted her gently, keeping hold of her in my arms. I danced with her in the moonlight that lit up the silver statues of angels so they stood out from the stone graves scattered in a circle around a huge flower bed in the eastern part of the cemetery. The wind in the branches of cypresses accompanied our dance with the applause of their feathery wooden hands rubbing against each other. We danced until almost dawn. Then I ran away with her, through the terraced fields that marked the side of the hill. We settled into a walk, blown along by the fresh morning breeze.

The next day I went back to the fisherman's house and found the boat ready for the trip, as he had promised. I didn't hesitate. I departed immediately, leaving behind me the anguish and despair felt during those long months of research and the weeks that followed her death. A new life was waiting for us somewhere on the blue sea.

White and puckering canvas sailed the sea while the west wind blew hard and adverse, as if to curse my departure. Our boat jumped nervously through the waves, slamming its belly on a sea hard as stone. Early in the day we were wrapped in a morning mist that would slowly dissolve, bringing with it large grey clouds, laden with water.

The horizon which at dawn looked uncertain on this route assigned to the whims of fate, would clear to resemble a curtain painted shades of blue on those cold spring mornings, as a rising sun sluiced yellow undertones to the flight of seagulls swirling around as they chased each other in play.

She would sit next to the captain's desk. Silent at the beginning of the trip, more and more talkative with the passing of those endless days we spent in the silence of the sea. Our solitude of hope would fade with the sunset, to be born again each new day.

I wandered for weeks, maybe months, without ever docking at a harbour. I was chasing a legend that I was convinced would materialise in front of my eyes, like a green island in the middle of the ocean.

One afternoon as I sat in the stern, I ran the palm of

my hand along its wooden rim to clean off the salt crystals. I felt them, so dense and hard they bit my fingers, as sharp as tailor's pins. The boat's reflection floated in the water. The wind filled the sails, puffing them out at irregular intervals, alternating in tune with my thoughts, more and more anguished as I watched her eyes smiling at me. There, from her chair. Her eyes were sweet, her mind hard. As always, convinced of her reasons. Determined and strong.

I got up, went to her, and stroked her head. I kissed her forehead as she squinted her eyes and hinted at a smile to repay my kindness.

Suddenly something hit the boat. I was thrown to the ground. Then, a second hit catapulted me out of the cabin. The sky immediately darkened. The blue colors of the sea turned into thick black brushstrokes. The waves swelled, straining up towards a leaden sky from which lightning shot down into the sea, sending out electric shocks across the surface.

The wind blew from many different directions, creating whirlpools that gnashed against the keel, sinking their teeth into the creaking wood of a vessel that suddenly looked like a wreck at the mercy of the waves. I tried to lower the sails. As I ran to the main mast, I saw that the patch of blue water, which shortly before had mirrored my ship, had now become an immense black carpet covering both water and sky and turning that paradise of color and light into a deep black hole. We were jumping about, thrown to the right and left. Then we were struck at both bow and stern at once by waves mighty and hard, walls of water crashing over us, like impossible mountains to climb.

That was when I lost control of the ship's wheel, and at that moment I felt I'd lost everything in my life. A wave threw me against the main mast as the ship tilted thirty degrees, rising over a wave. I slammed my head against the stern bench and my sight became blurred. Before losing consciousness, I saw another wave drag at us from the sea. The mouth of the furious storm was swallowing us whole.

When I woke up my love was gone. She had vanished into the air. Like that damnable storm, she'd been dispersed among the blue spots of a sky made up of clouds as fine as the dust of light beams. I screamed out her name, trying in vain to see her, but there was nothing to be done. The wind had stilled, the water was flat and blue, and silence enveloped me. The scene seemed as alive as a Renaissance painting, offering no hope in my passion to find her. After grabbing the oars, I continued to row in many different directions in that space that didn't seem to want to let me go. An invisible wall kept my navigation in a circular pattern while the compass went crazy, also circling without being able remain on any cardinal point. By nightfall, a full silver moon was the only celestial body I could see in a pale sky. I felt that even this natural force was about to abandon me, when another sudden and violent storm flooded the boat. It was as if this site that had been dominated by the deep blue, which stretched to infinity as if locked in a bubble, had suddenly been deleted. The storm threw me somewhere, into another part of the ocean.

I don't know how much time I spent at the mercy of the waves. I don't know how I managed to get out alive. When I opened my eyes I was not far from an island off the coast of Spain. The crew of a vessel returning from a fishing trip in the Atlantic had noticed my boat adrift and towed me to shore. The storm damage was so severe my boat could barely stay afloat.

One day I went back to the old fisherman. I went back to that island where I had begun my journey. I wanted this man to know about the blue vortex. About that infinity that he had dreamed of and I had seen, but not appreciated because I had been torn apart from my love. But the old man was no longer there.

I found the pub where we had met, and the bartender told me that he had left a few days after my departure. They had found him hanged in the shack where for years he had kept the boat. There was also a letter addressed to me, which the bartender had preserved. In that letter, which strangely did not smell of whiskey, the old fisherman had written a few lines:

'If you can't find the blue vortex, take care of my boat. Love it as I have loved it. Without it, I have nothing more to do.'

Words that marked me, passing on to me a task I could never ignore. From the old man I'd received a benediction and a curse. His lifeboat. And his doom.

I swear that when my time comes, I will go to the bottom and rest forever under the sea.

But for now ... my bottle is empty.

# Author Biography

Ferdinando Manzo is a professional journalist, born in the province of Napoli, Italy. He worked as an editor for an Italian Network for fifteen years, also collaborating as assistant producer to the production of TV programs.

He now lives in Sydney where he works as an editor for La Fiamma - Italian Media Corporation, author and song writer.

*L'UOMO CHE SALVÒ IL MONDO*, published in Italian, is Manzo's first novel. Arco: The Legend of the Blue Vortex is his first work in English.

Two collections of his poems, *Night Road to Life* and *The Dark Side of the Opera,* have been published by Sydney School of Arts & Humanities.

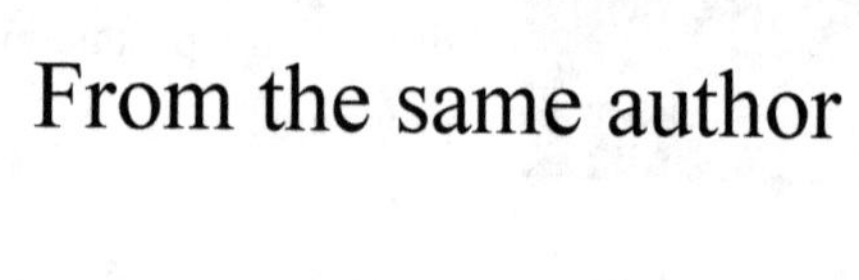

From the same author

# L'uomo che salvò il mondo
## (The man who saved the world)

L'uomo che salvò il mondo (The man who saved the world) is published in Italy by Lettere Animate editore. In his first novel, Ferdinando Manzo tells a post-apocalyptic story which takes place in a new world where survivors live divided between three cities: white, black and yellow, according to their race. The main character leaves his city with a mission to save the world. So begins an odyssey in which different destinies are woven together. There are stories of unhappiness and loneliness, with some twists. A sci-fi thriller outlining the final days of humanity.

**Category:** FICTION THRILLER/SCI-FI/POST-APOCALYPTIC

# Night Road to Life

Themes of the sea and the emotions, particularly the deeply felt joys and melancholies experienced by men, are a touchstone of NIGHT ROAD TO LIFE.

**Ferdinando Manzo**'s thoughts are not bound to fluidity; they fly to the greatest heights of exhilaration in poems such as, *The sky above us*, which displays 'a mantle of stars that burns in my heart' and in the evocative lines of *Eclipse*: 'the moon rose, bright between the eyelids of the night'. Even the constellation Andromeda is given due recognition, breaking her chains and ready for revenge, before another poem *The voice of the universe* explores 'a hidden legend as far away as waves in outer space'.

A distinctive quality of this collection of poems is its musicality – the sounds of words carefully chosen, and their rhythms. The pleasing effect of the sensuality of sounds, ranging from gentleness to the drama of sex, is in tune with the gamut of human emotion.

**Category**: POEMS

# The Dark Side of the Opera

In this collection, **Ferdinando Manzo** plays with language, teasing out meaning and tempting the senses. His poetic approach is akin to the Buddhist path where happiness is gained through an understanding of negation.

From the earthly to the stellar, each poem holds the reader in suspense until the final moment.

**Category**: POEMS

From the same publisher

# A Taste for Diamonds

A diamond theft. A fateful dancer. Passion, love and money in a story that unfolds through the rhythm of the tango.

'A Taste for Diamonds' is a love story that spans two continents, from London to Buenos Aires, as Harriett and the man she loves – the man who loves her in return – face the consequences of getting involved in the international diamond trade.

Not everyone's a good guy, as they find out to their peril.

Author **Diane Harding** plumbs the depths of romance and intrigue to bring readers a satisfying ending to a dangerous tale of love.

**Category:** BOOKS – MYSTERY – THRILLER – CRIME

# An extraordinary relationship

Early in **Leo Ryan**'s career as a counsellor he became aware of the number of female clients being abused by their husbands/partners/boyfriends and was determined to help.

This book highlights his conclusions, making it possible for most people to bring on the changes needed have a great relationship.

**Category**: NON-FICTION – HOW-TO BOOK – RELATION-SHIPS

# Burma My Mother
# And Why I Had To Leave

Myanmar's future is informed by its past - and BURMA MY MOTHER tells it like it is.

A valuable story of living through good times and plenty of bad in Burma, now known as Myanmar, before an escape to a new life of freedom.

Author **Sao Khemawadee Mangrai**'s husband, Hom, was imprisoned for 5 years, and his father was shot and killed sitting alongside independence leader, General Aung San, when he was assassinated.

Khemawadee grew up in a Shan state in the north-east of Myanmar, previously known as Burma, and now lives in Sydney. Her sad memories are also infused by the beauty of the country and the grace of Myanmar's Buddhist culture.

**Category**: MEMOIR

# Drenched by the Sun

I, who prophesy
by reading the stars and the wind,
now think of that country …

**Syam Sudhakar** 'has an eye for the strange and the uncanny and a way of building translucent metaphors,' according to leading South Indian poet, K. Satchidanandan.

An award-winning poet who writes in English and Malayalam, Sudhakar is based in Kerala, teaching and researching Indian poetry.

**Category**: POEMS

# I WILL

Unable to speak after suffering a stroke, **Jenny Sheldon** never lost her understanding of words.

Determined to regain her life, she used singing, swimming and her love of life to find her way back.
This book is her triumph – and a compelling example to others.

**Category**: MEMOIR

# Jiddu Krishnamurti World Philosopher
# Revised Edition

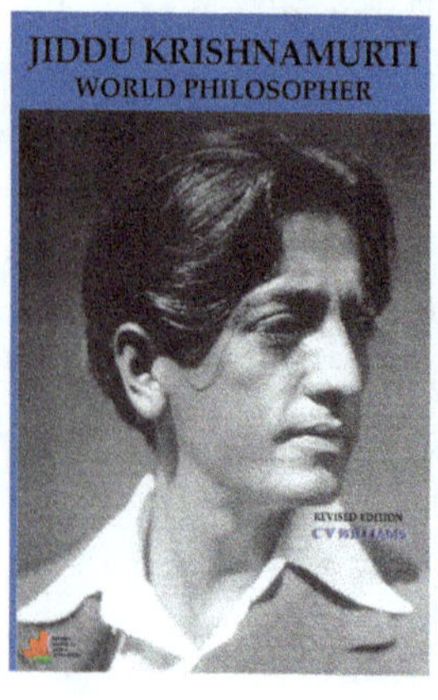



The life of the 20th-century philosopher Jiddu Krishnamurti was truly astonishing. As this new updated edition shows, people from all over the world would gather to hear him speak the wisdom of the ages.

Biographer **Christine (CV) Williams** carried out research over a period of four years to write this ebook account of Krishnamurti's life. She studied his major archive of personal correspondence and talks, and interviewed people who knew him intimately.

Krishna was born into poverty in a South Indian village, before being adopted by a wealthy English public figure, Annie Besant. As an adult he settled in California, travelling to India and England every year to give public lectures that inspired spiritual seekers beyond any single religion.

**Category:** BIOGRAPHY

# Reported Missing

**Di Harding**'s novel is set in a very contemporary Sydney, taking in multi-layered sights and sounds, from the northern beaches to performances at the Sydney Opera House.

What would you do if your daughter was missing and you thought your son-in-law was somehow involved? Is there someone who could help you, or would you take matters into your own hands?

She does, and so the terror begins – from vile and personal harassment to life threatening acts, until she is ready to commit murder.

Her obsession with killing grows in her mind until she begins to plan and plot. Can she actually do it? Then something shocking happens to make up her mind.

**Category**: DOMESTIC VIOLENCE
CRIME FICTION – SYDNEY NOVEL
AUSTRALIAN FICTION

# Road
# to Mandalay
# Less Travelled

'The Road to Mandalay Less Travelled' by **Ingrid Raj** provides research on a selection of Anglo-Burmese writing published from the period of British rule in Burma up until 2007.

What Raj shares with us in this study is the knowledge she gained about the value of social resistance achieved through writing. Both fiction and non-fiction texts are included in arguing a case that these might be viewed as tools of often ambivalent resistance against oppressive regimes, both local and colonial.Her research deserves a wider readership than was initially provided, and to this aim Sydney School of Arts & Humanities presents the work as its first publication in this new category of Essays & Theses.

**Category:** MEMOIR – LITERATURE – BURMA – HISTORY

# Road to Rishi Konda

'ROAD TO RISHI KONDA' by **Geetha Waters** is a memoir of insight and charm, with a serious educational purpose. The author recalls delightful and stimulating stories from her childhood to throw light on the work of the philosopher J. Krishnamurti as a revolutionary 20th century educator.

At once fascinating and enchanting, Geetha Waters' stories centre on a girl growing up in Kerala and Andhra Pradesh in the '60s and '70s.

These youthful tales are underpinned by Geetha's deep understanding of childhood education, based both on her academic studies and in practice in her daily life as a mother and childcare professional.

Written from a child's perspective, the tales of awakening to life offer the reader an opportunity to appreciate how all children learn, as they draw on a deep well of curiosity that needs to be respected.

**Category**: BIOGRAPHY & AUTOBIOGRAPHY
PERSONAL MEMOIR – EDUCATORS

# Stranger

Political journalist Nick Hunter suddenly loses his memory. He can't find his wallet, his computer password or even his name. When it comes to women it's even more confusing. Does he have a lover or a wife?

It doesn't get any easier when he realises his life is in danger as he's been researching a story on corruption at the highest level of political life. Things get even stickier once Nick has a 6-shooter out of his safety deposit box and in his hand, ready to fire in his own defence.

Set in the northern and eastern suburbs of Sydney where coffee and sex are almost too freely available, this story will sharpen your senses and set your crime thriller compass on true course.

**Category**: FICTION – CRIME

# The Boots

All Mike has to do is get his mate's lucky boots to the stadium – but when Mike accidentally loses them his day is turned upside down.
Will he find them – and if so, will it be in time for the game?

In trying to meet the deadline, Mike has to cope with weekend crowds, hamburger cravings, a girl with a fox tattoo, Jedi Knights, and a bunch of footie supporters who are hell bent on getting their hands on those lucky boots.

Mike always thought Karma was a myth. But he may just become a believer.

**Category**: FICTION – ACTION & ADVENTURE
SPORTS & RECREATION – RUGBY LEAGUE

# Waking the Mind

**Geetha Waters**' engaging selection of short stories, 'Waking the Mind', is a reflection on Jiddu Krishnamurti's impact on her education based on her experiences at a school he founded in South India.

Geetha credits her passion for inquiry as being sparked the first time she heard Krishnamurti speak when she was six. That talk at the Rishi Valley School set her on an intriguing course of inquiry into the mysterious nature of the mind, the vitality of the natural world, and a creative understanding of life.

Geetha Waters also incorporates the stories found in 'Road to Rishi Konda' in the STEP program for children and teachers in South India, a training module based on Krishnamurti's interactive style of relating with children.

**Category:** NON-FICTION – INDIAN STORIES
PHILOSOPHY KRISHNAMURTI

# What's in a Name?
## 20 People - 20 Stories

This collection of short stories will appeal to readers who are attracted to snapshots of the human condition. While set in Australia, the stories reflect universal themes. They range over a number of genres from crime to science fiction, from human weakness to human strength, and capture pockets of life with uncanny accuracy and sensitivity.

The author, **Lawrence Goodstone**, is a retired public servant who spent his professional life writing for others. With a background ranging from teaching to immigrant services as well as assisting in the delivery of the 2000 Olympic Games in Sydney, he is now in a position to write for himself and create stories from a life well lived.

**Category:** FICTION – SHORT STORY – SYDNEY STORIES
AUSTRALIAN FICTION